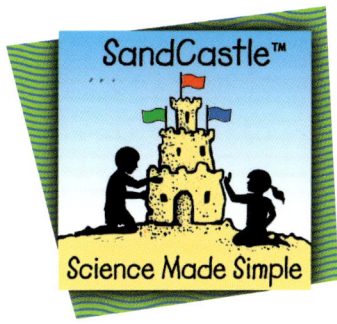

It's a Date, Let's Investigate!

Kelly Doudna

Consulting Editors, Diane Craig, M.A./Reading Specialist
and Susan Kosel, M.A. Education

Published by ABDO Publishing Company, 4940 Viking Drive, Edina, Minnesota 55435.

Copyright © 2007 by Abdo Consulting Group, Inc. International copyrights reserved in all countries. No part of this book may be reproduced in any form without written permission from the publisher. SandCastle™ is a trademark and logo of ABDO Publishing Company.

Printed in the United States.

Credits
Edited by: Pam Price
Curriculum Coordinator: Nancy Tuminelly
Cover and Interior Design and Production: Mighty Media
Photo Credits: AbleStock, BananaStock Ltd., Comstock, Creatas, Kelly Doudna, Image Source, ShutterStock, Wewerka Photography

Library of Congress Cataloging-in-Publication Data

Doudna, Kelly, 1963-
   It's a date, let's investigate! / Kelly Doudna.
     p. cm. -- (Science made simple)
   ISBN 10 1-59928-596-7 (hardcover)
   ISBN 10 1-59928-597-5 (paperback)

   ISBN 13 978-1-59928-596-2 (hardcover)
   ISBN 13 978-1-59928-597-9 (paperback)
   1. Science--Methodology--Juvenile literature. 2. Science--Experiments--Juvenile literature. I. Title.
II. Series: Science made simple (ABDO Publishing Company)

Q175.2.D68 2007
507.2--dc22
                                                                                                       2006012569

SandCastle Level: Fluent

SandCastle™ books are created by a professional team of educators, reading specialists, and content developers around five essential components—phonemic awareness, phonics, vocabulary, text comprehension, and fluency—to assist young readers as they develop reading skills and strategies and increase their general knowledge. All books are written, reviewed, and leveled for guided reading, early reading intervention, and Accelerated Reader® programs for use in shared, guided, and independent reading and writing activities to support a balanced approach to literacy instruction. The SandCastle™ series has four levels that correspond to early literacy development. The levels help teachers and parents select appropriate books for young readers.

Emerging Readers
(no flags)

Beginning Readers
(1 flag)

Transitional Readers
(2 flags)

Fluent Readers
(3 flags)

These levels are meant only as a guide. All levels are subject to change.

To **investigate** means to find out more about something. When you investigate, you ask questions, do experiments, and use other scientific skills to discover information.

Words used to talk about investigating:
**conclusion
hypothesis
inquiry
question
test**

An **investigation** begins with a ???.

What things will a  pick up?

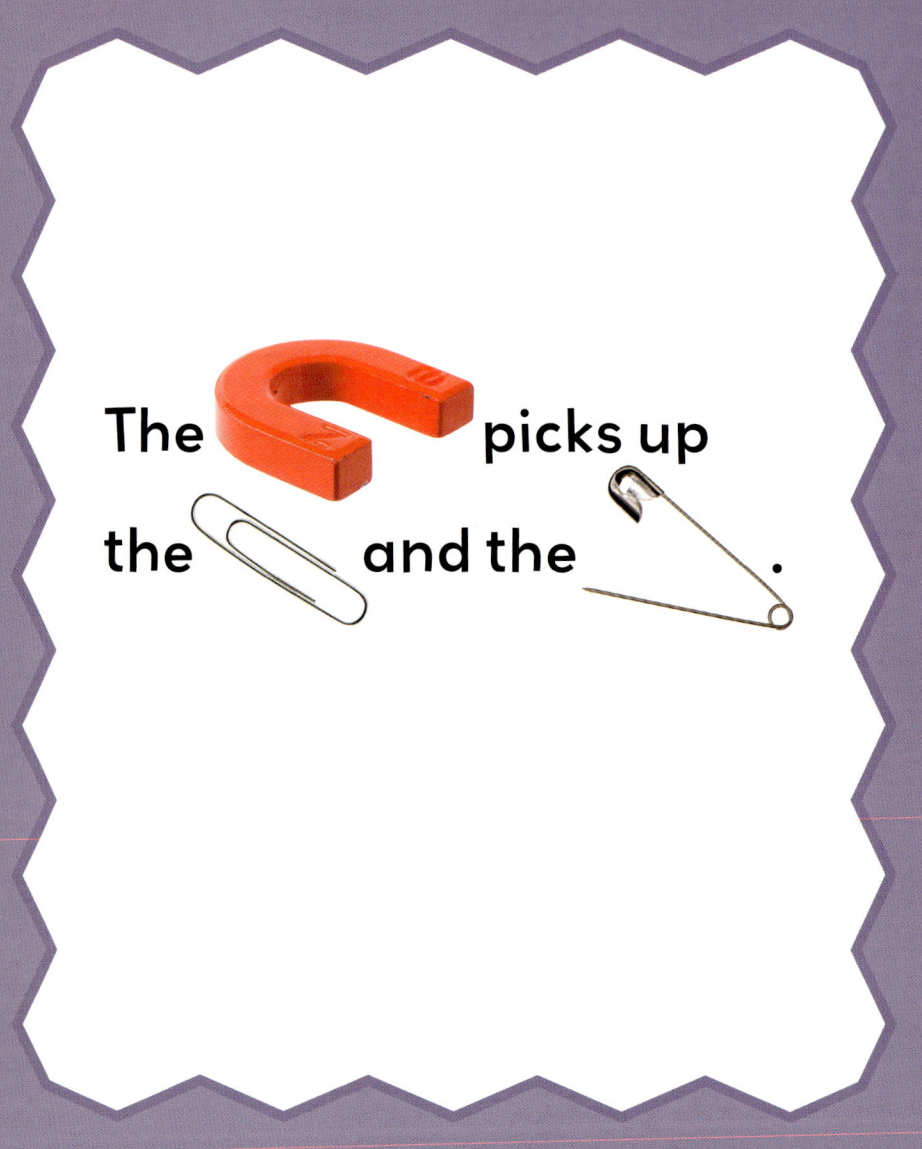

The 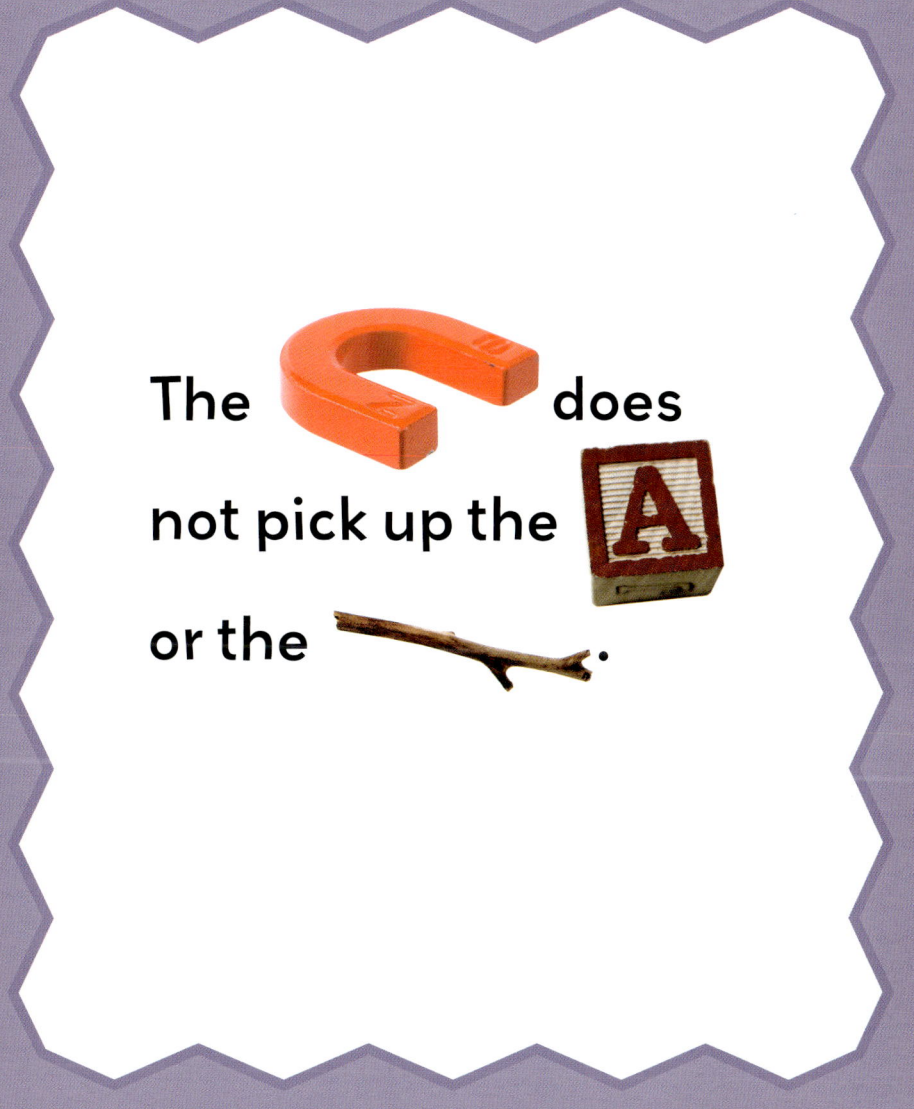 does not pick up the A or the ⌒.

I **conclude** that the  does not pick up  .

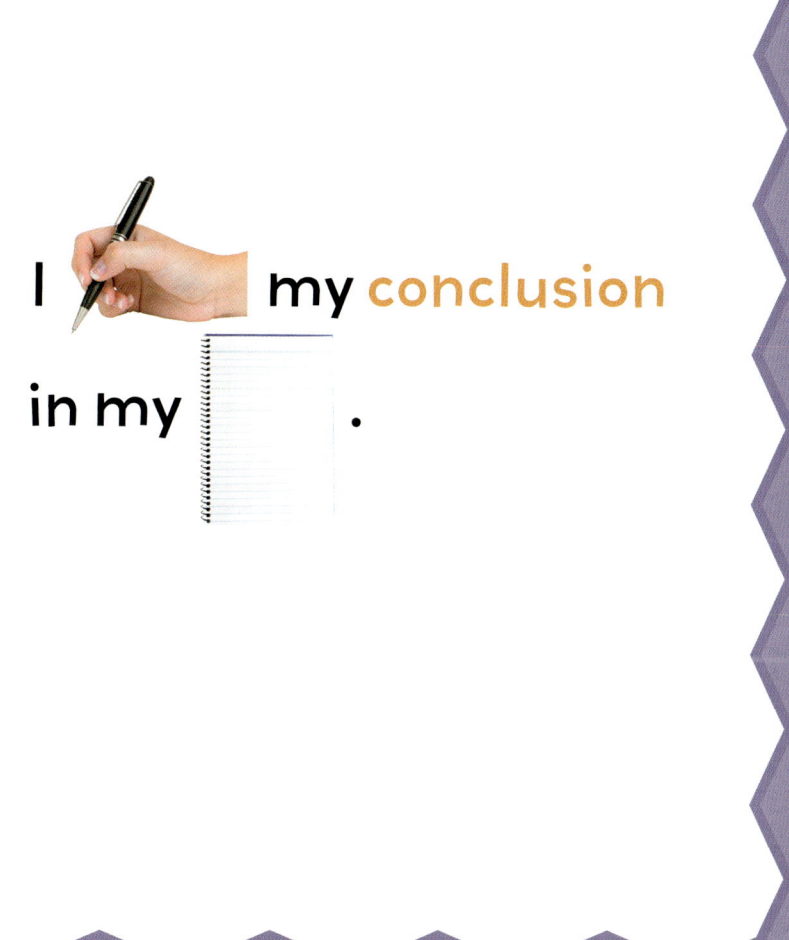

It's a Date, Let's Investigate!

Nate has a **question**, so he starts an **investigation**. He forms a **hypothesis**, and then he tests this notion.

Will the wet or the dry towel have better luck holding the duck?

Nate goes on a quest to perform a fair test. When the test is done, he draws a conclusion.

The dry towel is stronger and holds the ducks longer.

The inquiry comes to an end, and Nate writes down what happened. Nate thinks it's great to investigate!

> The wet towel tore, and the dry towel held more.

We Can Investigate Every Day!

Abby, Amy, and Deb want to know if the green, orange, and pink frostings taste different from each other.

Each girl will taste each color of frosting. Then they will share their conclusions.

Andy is curious to know if the size of the bead affects how fast it moves along the wires.

Andy lets a large bead go and records how long it takes to slide down the wire. Then he does the same with a small bead.

Dan wonders if he will make the biggest bubble by blowing hard or gently.

To find out, Dan blows hard on the bubble wand. Then he blows gently.

Mia wants to know what kind of food the birds like best.

What steps should Mia take in her *investigation*?

Glossary

conclusion – a judgment made after reasoning and thinking carefully.

experiment – a scientific test done to discover information.

hypothesis – a statement that seems to explain a set of facts and is the basis for an experiment.

inquiry – an investigation.

notion – an idea or opinion about something.